I0547895

HICCUP'S HICCUPS
DOUBLE BUBBLE

Dr. J. Alvarez

Tri House Books

The opinions expressed in this manuscript are solely the opinions of the author and do not represent the opinions or thoughts of the publisher. The author has represented and warranted full ownership and/or legal right to publish all the materials in this book.

Double Bubble
Hiccup's Hiccups
All Rights Reserved.
Copyright © 2016, 2017 Dr. J. Alvarez
v2.0 r2.2

Cover Illustrations © 2016, 2017 Outskirts Press, Inc.
All rights reserved - used with permission.

Tri House Books

ISBN: 978-0-578-17752-6

Library of Congress Control Number: 2015921413

PRINTED IN THE UNITED STATES OF AMERICA

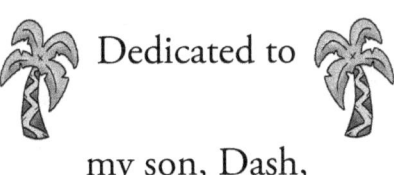 Dedicated to

my son, Dash,

for teaching me that

laughter is the best medicine

for keeping a positive outlook.

Table of Contents

CHAPTER 1
I'm Naked!

Tibby the Chubby Tiger, Benny the Bumblebee, and Hiccup the Hippo were the best of friends. But sometimes, a friend can be totally annoying.

Tibby was in a deep sleep. He was snoring like a bear.

Benny was trying to take a nap on Tibby's fluffy, furry belly, but he could not sleep with all that snoring: *"Zzzzzz-huggghh… zzzzzz-huggghh… snort-snort."*

Hiccup yelled out to Benny who was a little away, "I can hear him from here. I don't know how you can be with him—*hiccup*—with all that noise. Tibby's snoring sounds like a wounded pig—*hiccup*." Hiccup's words were broken up by her hiccups. Yes, she hiccupped when she spoke. And when she was nervous about something, she hiccupped even more—sometimes with four hiccups in a row.

Benny was annoyed. "I'm not sure how I do it. I try to wake him up, but then, he wakes up with droopy eyes for a couple of seconds, and it's back to more snoring."

Hiccup walked over to Benny. "We've got to do something about this."

Benny had tried all kinds of things to get Tibby to stop snoring. He had put his hands over his ears, but Tibby's snores were too loud. He had asked Hiccup to push Tibby on his side to help him breathe easier and stop snoring, but Tibby kept rolling back. And although this sounds disgusting, one time, Benny had been so desperate for Tibby to stop snoring that he tried to unclog his nose. Tibby had a horrible cold, and he was snoring louder than usual. He needed something to clean Tibby's nose with. So, he found a long stick with smooth sides and peeked inside Tibby's nose. He was disgusted by what he saw, but something had to be done. He slowly started to do a little nose cleaning. He began to swab the goo and then flick it off. But when he was doing so, Benny's fuzz gently brushed the tip of Tibby's nose hair. Unexpectedly, Benny felt mild tremors where he stood near Tibby's nose. Benny knew exactly what was going to happen. He tried to back away, but it was too late. Tibby had violently sneezed him out.

Shuddering at the memory, Benny asked, "Hiccup, what else could we do?"

Hiccup said, "Well, for starters, why

don't you—*hiccup*—just walk away?"

"Hiccup, you know my fuzz is way too heavy—so heavy that it keeps me from flying. Tibby is like my wings, and he gets me around. If I leave him, then I might get stuck somewhere," said Benny.

"What about a haircut, Benny? We can get rid of some of that fuzz," said Hiccup.

Though a haircut would probably work for anyone else, there was a problem with this idea. Benny was small, and it would be hard to give him a haircut without hurting him.

Hiccup and Benny sat there, trying to think of something.

Hiccup said, "Benny, I know—*hiccup*—what we could do. I've always had a little too much hair on my upper lip… and some fuzz around my belly button. You know a girl always wants to be smooth-a-licious. So, I wax it off. We can wax the hair off you too!"

With a look of terror, Benny replied, "That sounds painful. Who does something like that?"

"A bumblebee who wants to fly, that's who. It's easy, and it doesn't hurt at all," said Hiccup.

What Benny did not know was that hippos have very thick skin, much thicker than most animals. And that meant when Hiccup waxed herself, she didn't feel a thing.

Benny said, "Well, if it doesn't hurt, then let's try it. I've always wondered what I would look like without any fuzz."

Hiccup picked Benny up and put him on her shoulder. She grabbed her coconut shell and a stick and found some tree sap to pour inside the coconut shell. Then, she placed the shell in the sun to heat up the wax. After that, she and Benny hunted for some fresh leaves to use as waxing strips.

Hiccup said, "Let's get this over with."

Hiccup slowly put the tree sap all over Benny. Then, she laid the fresh leaves on him and told him, "This won't hurt—*hiccup*—a bit. Just relax."

Benny inhaled deeply and braced himself, because now, he was starting to have a bad feeling.

Hiccup counted, "One. Two. THREE!" and then ripped the leaves off very quickly. Benny let out a giant yelp. Everything was starting to swirl. He saw spots before his eyes. "I THOUGHT THIS WASN'T SUPPOSED TO HURT!"

All the commotion woke up Tibby. When he came over, he could not believe what he saw. There were uneven tufts of fuzz at many spots, making Benny look like a disheveled cat who was perhaps tossed in the tumble drier.

Hiccup realized that she had missed some spots. She quickly slapped another layer of tree sap and laid some more leaves on Benny.

"Oh no, no, NO!" said Benny. Before he could say another word, Hiccup ripped the leaves off him again.

"OUCH!" shrieked Benny.

Relieved that it was all over, Benny slowly uncovered his eyes and with hesitation asked his friends, "So, how do I look?"

Taking a gulp of air, Hiccup said, "Well, it's certainly a different look. I think you should—*hiccup—hiccup—hiccup—hiccup*—take a look for yourself."

Tibby was a little confused about what was going on. He was wondering what happened to Benny's fuzz. Hiccup explained that Tibby's snoring was driving Benny crazy and he needed to get away from it. They wanted to see if Benny would be able to fly without his hair.

Tibby, Hiccup, and Benny walked over

to a small pond. Benny looked into the water at his reflection and was horrified. He yelled, "I'M NAKED! I LOOK LIKE A HAIRLESS CAT!"

"It's not that bad," said Tibby with a funny look.

"YES, IT IS!" cried Benny.

Hiccup said, "Well, let's look on the brighter side. Maybe you can fly now."

"Yes, maybe you can fly," said Tibby.

Tibby picked Benny up, and yes, he was much lighter. Tibby held him up and told him that if for some reason he could not fly, he would catch him. Benny was as nervous as a baby bird taking his first flight. Tibby then threw him high into the air. At first, Benny plunged down a little… and then… off he flew. He was really flying. He felt the wind against his face. He was swooping down and then soaring up.

Tibby and Hiccup just smiled.

CHAPTER 2
Please Say Yes.
Please Say No.

Before Benny lost all his fuzz, he was always with Tibby. Now, Benny was hardly around. Hiccup could tell that Tibby was a little lonely, and she was up to something.

"Hey Tibby, you always talk about Charlize the Swift-Footed Cheetah. Without Benny—*hiccup*—around all the time, you can finally ask her out on a date," said Hiccup with a smile.

Every time Tibby heard the name

Charlize, his heart went *pit-a-pat, pit-a-pat, pitty-pat, pitty-pat*. His palms started to sweat. His mouth started to feel dry. Just the thought of asking Charlize on a date put Tibby's tongue in a twist.

"Hiccup, I can't do it," said Tibby.

Hiccup could see that Tibby was going to back out. "Come on, Tibby. There's no need to be this nervous."

"I feel like my heart is going to pop out of my chest," said Tibby nervously.

Hiccup laughed. "You'll be fine."

"Hiccup, I can't get it together. When I talk to her, I say the strangest things, like… 'My stomach gets bloated after eating too many coconuts'," said Tibby.

Looking at Tibby with sincere eyes, Hiccup told him, "My, my, Tibby. You've got it bad."

While Hiccup was putting a plan together to get Tibby to ask Charlize out, Benny had taken a break from flying. He was lying down and soaking up some sun. He could hear Hiccup and Tibby chatting. And then, upon faintly hearing the name Charlize, his eyes widened. He lifted his head and listened very closely. What Tibby did not know was that Benny did not want anyone to take away his best friend. Benny did not like this idea at all.

Under his breath, he said, "Charlize that, Charlize this—Charlize, Charlize, Charlize! I can't stand to hear that name anymore."

Benny yelled out, "HEY TIBBY, WOMEN ARE NOTHING BUT TROUBLE. SAVE YOURSELF A LIFE OF MISERY, AND DON'T ASK HER OUT!"

With a stern voice, Hiccup said, "BENNY!" and then gave him the sort of look a mother would give her child when they are about to do something very bad. Then, she looked at Tibby and said, "Don't

listen to him. I don't know what has gotten into him."

Tibby said, "I will do it tomorrow."

"You're not going to get—*hiccup*—out of this one. If you don't do it today, I will drag you myself to her… and I'm bigger than you," said Hiccup.

"All right, Hiccup," said Tibby with frustration.

So Tibby and Hiccup started to walk toward the waterhole. Benny did not want to be left behind, so he flew onto Tibby's shoulder. For the moment, Tibby was so happy that Benny was back with him. On the way, Tibby picked a delicious, sweet fireball melon to ease his nervousness.

He said, "There's nothing like a fireball melon to lift your spirits," and cracked it open and drank the juice. Then, he used his claws to cut out pieces and ate them for a snack.

Right before they got there, Hiccup picked some flowers that Tibby could offer to Charlize.

From a distance, Tibby could see Charlize. He started to pump himself up, like he was going into a big fight. "I can do this," said Tibby gruffly to himself. He licked his palms to slick his hair back, stuck out his chest, and proceeded in his best manly walk.

"How do I look, Hiccup?" asked Tibby.

"Great! But get rid of that ridiculous walk," said Hiccup. She then grabbed Benny off Tibby's shoulder and told him, "You're staying—*hiccup*—with me."

Hiccup was watching with excitement and was quietly cheering Tibby on. Benny, on the other hand, was looking at Tibby as if he was the enemy's battleship and hoping Charlize would fire cannons at him and sink him.

"I hope Charlize says yes," said Hiccup.

"I hope Charlize says no," said Benny quietly.

Tibby was finally right in front of Charlize. He stared at her for a couple of seconds and finally said, "Hi, Charlize."

"Hi, Tibby," responded Charlize.

"Got some flowers for you," said Tibby, handing them.

Charlize smiled. "They're beautiful."

Tibby looked at Charlize's sparkling eyes, but all that came out of his mouth was "Uh, uh… *meow*."

"Tibby, you're nervous. What is it?" said Charlize.

There was a long silence and finally Tibby said, "Will you go on a date with me? I want to take you by the waterfall and watch the rainbows."

Hiccup and Benny could barely hear them.

"Benny, she's going to say yes. I can see it

16

in her face," said Hiccup with adoring eyes.

Looking at Hiccup, Benny said with panic, "NO, NO, NO! THIS CAN'T HAPPEN!"

"Too late. I just heard her say yes," said a smiling Hiccup.

With a frown, Benny said, "Oh, no. This is the worst day of my life."

Benny the Bumblebee was not happy. He was so mad at himself for ignoring Tibby all those days. He used to love how he would sit on Tibby's shoulder and fly high as he leaped into the air. Now, he felt as if his best friend was being taken away from him. He was very, very jealous. Jealousy is an unhappy feeling and can happen when we think an outsider is taking away someone we care about. Sometimes, we may say very unkind words or behave unkindly when we are jealous, and Benny decided he will behave quite the same towards Charlize because of how he felt.

CHAPTER 3
Split in Two

Hiccup noticed that Benny was not his usual self, and she was pretty sure she knew the reason for this. She wanted to do something to get Benny's mind off the whole Charlize thing. She wanted to do something that would involve just her, Benny, and Tibby.

"Tibby, why don't we—*hiccup*—go on another adventure?" said Hiccup with a giggle.

Hiccup wanted to use her magical hiccups to take them on an adventure to another place. Every time Hiccup hiccupped underwater, she created a bubble that was really a doorway to other new places. Hiccup called these doorways "portals."

With a great big smile, Hiccup said, "Tibby, tell Benny we're heading to the waterhole to open a portal."

Hiccup, Tibby, and Benny arrived at the waterhole, which was on the desert side of Coconut Desert Island. Coconut Desert Island was like no other island; it was half-tropical rainforest and half-desert. Tibby, Benny, and Hiccup mainly stayed on the tropical side of the island, but Hiccup liked to go to the waterhole to open portals because that was where she had been opening portals since she was Little Hiccup.

Hiccup got into the waterhole. She looked around to make sure no one else was there, but there was someone there. It was Charlize the Swift-Footed Cheetah. She

Where is Coconut Desert Island?

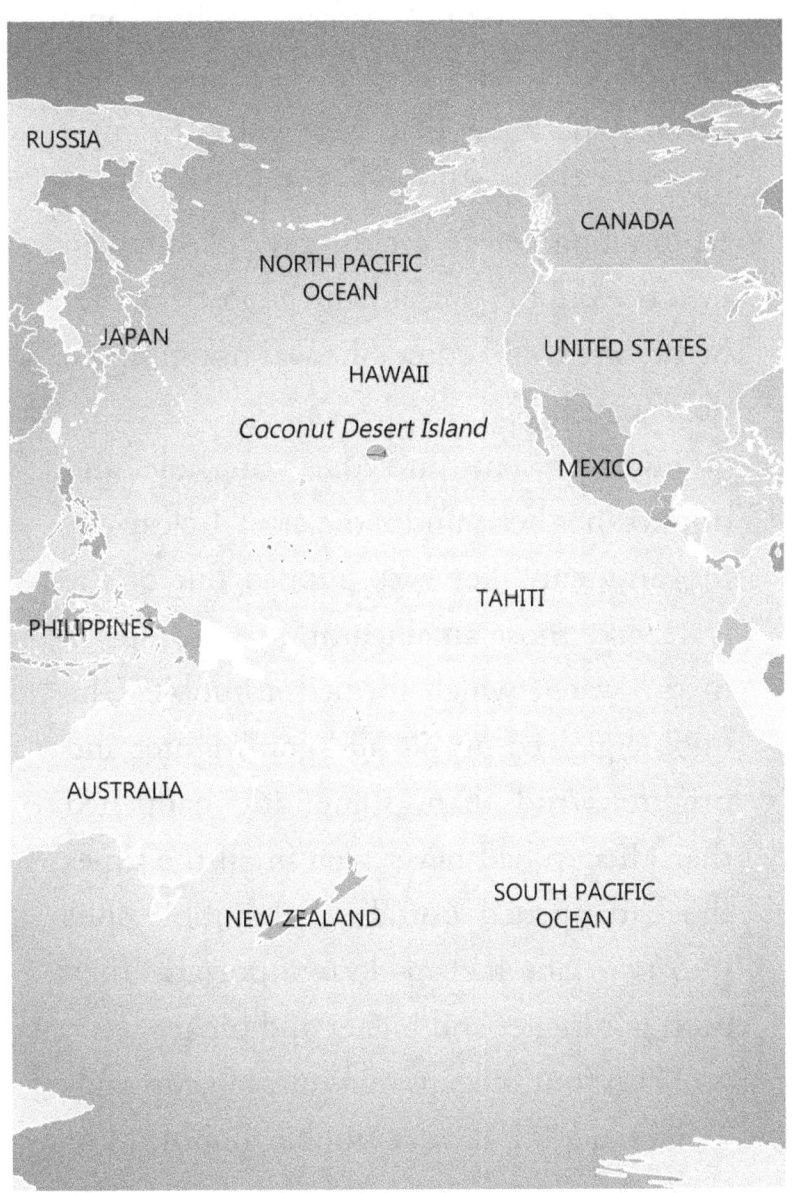

was secretly looking on from behind some bushes. Charlize had seen Hiccup do this before. She knew they were going to enter a portal. The last time they did it, she waited too long before deciding to follow them into the bubble portal, which closed on her before she could enter. She was not going to do that again.

Hiccup went into the waterhole and dunked her head under the crystal-clear water. Suddenly, her eyes popped out of the water like those an alligator. She hiccupped in the water, which formed a bubble. The bubble glowed purple and got brighter and brighter. And then, something happened that Hiccup had never seen in all the times she had opened portals. The bubble split into two. She had made two portals. They both got bigger and bigger and bigger.

With four hiccups in a row, Hiccup said, "That's odd. I have a double bubble. I've never been able to make two portals at one time."

Tibby said, "THIS IS TOTALLY AWESOME! Which door do you want to go through, guys?"

With excitement, Benny said, "Let's go to the one on the right!"

"I like the one on the left. Look how—*hiccup*—much brighter that portal is on the left," said Hiccup.

Tibby laughed. "I wonder what would happen if I put one foot in the right and one foot in the left."

"Don't be silly," said Hiccup.

Tibby said, "I'm going to enter with style. I'm going to spin myself up to the portals and then leap into one."

As Tibby prepared himself for his grand entrance into one of the portals, Charlize was looking on. She was not about to miss this. Her eyes were stuck on Tibby and

Hiccup, and nothing was going to distract her. Then, all of a sudden, she heard a loud buzzing sound. It was a giant green beetle, and it had landed on a rock in front of her. Charlize let out a squeal. As she was trying to get away from the beetle, Tibby started to slowly spin himself. Benny was sitting on his head, and he was hanging on tight. And then, Tibby's spins got faster and faster. He was getting closer to the portals. Benny's world was starting to spin. Everything was becoming a blur. He closed his eyes, which made it worse. Now, he was starting to get very dizzy—so dizzy that he started to lose his grip.

As Tibby made his final spin, he whipped his head from right to left, and Benny was flung into the portal on the *left*. Then, Tibby dramatically leaped into the portal on the *right*. Hiccup saw Tibby's dramatic entrance into the portal, and she followed him in.

In the meantime, Charlize finally got rid of the beetle. When she looked up, Tibby, Benny, and Hiccup were no longer there. She was pretty sure out of the corner of her eye, she saw Tibby and Hiccup enter the *right* portal. As she was going to take a step into the *right* portal, Charlize heard that same loud buzzing sound. It was the giant green beetle… AGAIN. She turned and took a step back. She began waving it off with her hand, but the beetle kept coming at her.

"WHY DON'T YOU GO AWAY?" shouted Charlize. Then, she took a big step backwards and realized she was in the *left* portal. When she got to the other side, she saw rolling green hills covered with tall, thick grass. A stream with trees and bushes along the sides was running through the land. She also saw Benny standing by the stream.

With a gloomy look, Benny said, "Oh,

great! Of all the animals, I'm stuck with you! Tibby had to spin me right off into this portal… WITH… YOU."

In a soft voice, Charlize said, "I know you don't like me."

With arrogance, Benny said, "It's a good thing I can fly, because I'm going to fly away from you."

As Charlize saw Benny fly away, she was sad. And frankly, she did not know what she had done to Benny. All she knew was that Benny had not been very nice to her.

CHAPTER 4
Paul the
Paranoid Snake

Tibby finally found Hiccup. Wherever they were, it reminded them of their home on Coconut Desert Island. The portal they entered took them to a magnificent tropical rainforest. The rainforest was very lush with lots of green plants, except this rainforest had huge mountain evergreens, which could be seen at a distance. Looking out, Tibby and Hiccup could see a thick mist starting to disappear over the forest floor, and the trees were starting to appear.

"I feel right at home," said Tibby.

"Tibby. Hey, Tibby. Do you notice that you're missing someone?" said Hiccup, pointing to the top of his head.

Tibby inattentively replied, "Nope."

Hiccup stressed, "*Tibby, where's Benny?*"

Tibby slowly rolled his eyes upward, and then, he gently patted his head. "I DON'T KNOW!" With panic, Tibby started looking around. "BENNY! BENNY! WHERE ARE YOU?" He stopped to listen but could hear only parrots, a howling monkey, and croaking frogs.

"I don't think he's here," replied Hiccup.

Tibby called out again. "BENNY, BENNY! WHERE ARE YOU?" But this time, he heard a *hiss*. Then, he heard it again.

"Hiccup, do you hear that?" said Tibby.

"Yes! *Hiccup—hiccup—hiccup—hiccup.* What is it?" replied Hiccup.

Tibby and Hiccup were just staring at it,

and they were not sure if they should move. They were looking at a huge snake. He was taller than Hiccup. Hiccup screamed, and four more hiccups came out. Then, a funny thing happened. The snake screamed. Then, Tibby screamed and jumped into Hiccup's arms. The snake screamed again and put his tail over his eyes. He turned his head the other way.

"Wait a minute," said Hiccup. "Are you afraid of us?"

"Yes," said the frightened snake.

"Have you seen yourself?" said Tibby. He looked at Hiccup and quietly told her, "He is way bigger than any snake we have ever seen on Coconut Desert Island. I think I'm going to pee myself."

Hiccup gave Tibby a look that said, "*Get it together.*" Then, with sincere eyes, she looked at the snake and said, "We won't hurt you. I'm Hiccup the Hippo, and this is

my friend, Tibby the Chubby Tiger."

With his head down, the snake said, "I'm Paul the Paranoid Snake."

"Paranoid? What does that mean?" asked Tibby.

Paul said, "When you're paranoid, you worry that everyone is out to get you. My dad used to call me paranoid when I was young because I was afraid of everything, and the name has stuck ever since."

Tibby said, "My mom used to call me chubby when I was a cub, and it really hurt my feelings. Then, everyone else started calling me chubby, and that name has stuck ever since."

"But Paul, you look like the most dangerous—*hiccup*—snake I have ever seen," said Hiccup.

Paul looked about in panic, and then frantically said, "They're coming! The lights! The animals! They're all coming for me!"

Tibby asked, "Who's coming for you?"

Right then and there, Hiccup heard another *hiss*. "Hey, Paul! Did you bring any friends with you?"

"No!" said Paul fearfully.

It was another snake. The snake screamed with terror once he saw Paul. "IT'S A KING COBRA!"

"It's all right," Hiccup said calmly. "He's a nice snake… really he is… could you please tell us what you know about king cobras?"

The snake calmed down a little. In a firm voice, he said, "I'm warning you guys. If you want to live, RUN as fast as you can. They're good swimmers, and they can climb trees fast. I've seen an elephant take her last breath after one of those guys bit her. They will stand tall before they spit poison out of their fangs. I've seen one spit directly into the eyes of another snake. It's a snake killer, and I don't plan to be his next meal." The snake slithered off as fast as he could and disappeared into the forest floor.

Hiccup said, "Paul, you are a dangerous snake. You're not just a snake, and you're not just a cobra, but you're a KING COBRA."

Paul said, "They're coming for me."

"Didn't you just say that, Paul? Now, who's coming for you?" asked Tibby.

Paul cringed in fear. Trembling, he said, "They're coming for me. The lights. The animals. They're all flashing before my eyes."

"Paul, there's nobody here but ants," said Hiccup.

"RED ANTS!" said Paul. "Those are the worst. They can pick things up way bigger than them… like me. They're as powerful as Superman. There are thousands and thousands of them. They can pick me up, take me to a hut, and burn me alive."

Hiccup said, "Paul, don't you think— *hiccup*—that's a bit extreme, over the top?"

"No. I have seen some ants eat a cricket. It was an awful sight," said Paul.

Tibby and Hiccup knew they had to help Paul, but how?

CHAPTER 5
Return of the Fuzz

Meanwhile, Benny was starting to feel heavier. He realized that his fuzz was starting to grow back. Benny was barely flying above the ground now. He had to stop flying because he was so tired. He found a nice shady tree and under the tree was a leaf. Closing his eyes, he softly said, "This leaf isn't as soft as Tibby, but it will have to do." Then, he fell asleep.

When Benny woke up, he tried to fly again, but it was no use. He could not fly very high. He was stuck. "Now what am I going to do?" said Benny quietly.

As he was walking with his head down, he knew he was going to be in trouble. He was right. From afar, he saw a bird. This was not a bird he had seen before. It was a beautiful, colorful bird, but it was not as nice as it looked. It was a bee-eater bird. These birds usually wore a black robber's mask and darted across the sky to catch their next meal… and they loved to eat bumblebees.

The bee-eater bird was getting closer. Benny started to frantically look for a place to hide… but it was too late. The bee-eater bird and Benny were eye to eye. Benny was too scared to move.

The bird walked up to Benny slowly and said with an evil voice, "My, you look extra plump."

Benny took a big gulp of air, and his voice cracked. "I'm really not that plump. I've just got a lot of extra fuzz. I'm actually a skinny twig, and I wouldn't be much of a snack."

The bird got even closer. Benny closed his eyes and waited for the bird to take him. All he kept thinking about was that he was not going to be able to say goodbye to Tibby. He was also thinking about how jealous he was and how mean he had been to Charlize.

Thinking this was the end, Benny heard a clap and someone hallooing at the bird. "GET OUT OF HERE, BIRD!" a voice yelled. The bird was frightened away. It was Charlize, and she had saved Benny's life. "I was looking all over for you, Benny."

Benny was so relieved and happy to see Charlize, but he was also sad because he could not fly anymore.

Charlize bent down and picked Benny up.

Benny looked at Charlize with sad eyes and told her, "I'm really sorry, Charlize, that I was so mean to you. I thought you were

going to take my best friend away."

Charlize said, "Oh, Benny. I'm not taking anyone away from Tibby. I like to be around him as much as you. We can all spend time together." Then, she placed Benny on her shoulder, just like Tibby did.

Benny said, "Charlize, I must say, you are much softer than Tibby."

"Thanks, Benny, but I can't climb high through the trees like Tibby," said Charlize.

Benny just smiled.

"Now, I'm not sure if we're going to get back to Coconut Desert Island, but in case Tibby and Hiccup try to look for us, we have to leave clues," said a worried Charlize.

Benny told Charlize that they should go back to the spot where the portal had opened and backtrack their steps. They did just that.

"Now, let's leave clues," said Benny.

Charlize asked, "What do you think we

should do?"

Benny told Charlize they could lay branches and rocks around to make arrows, showing which way they went. Just maybe Hiccup might be able to make a portal to wherever they were, and just maybe they might see the arrows and find them.

"We might be stuck together. We may never get back to Coconut Desert Island," said Charlize.

"I know, but at least we have each other," said Benny. "Now, we should find a place to stay. What do you say?"

Benny learned a very important lesson that day. Jealousy can be felt when we think someone is taking someone we care about away from us. Benny thought Charlize was taking his best friend away. What he learned was that both Charlize and he made Tibby happy. Besides, just maybe the person we are jealous of might become a good friend to us.

CHAPTER 6
A New Title

Hiccup was looking around and then asked Paul, "Now that I think about it, where are we?"

Paul said, "You're in Noodle Toes in China."

Tibby gave Paul a funny look and asked, "Why do you call it Noodle Toes?"

Paul explained that the raindrops here fell in different sizes. Some looked like long noodles and some looked like giant big toes.

Tibby said, "Those must be some weird-looking raindrops. Ours are just... round."

Where is Noodle Toes?

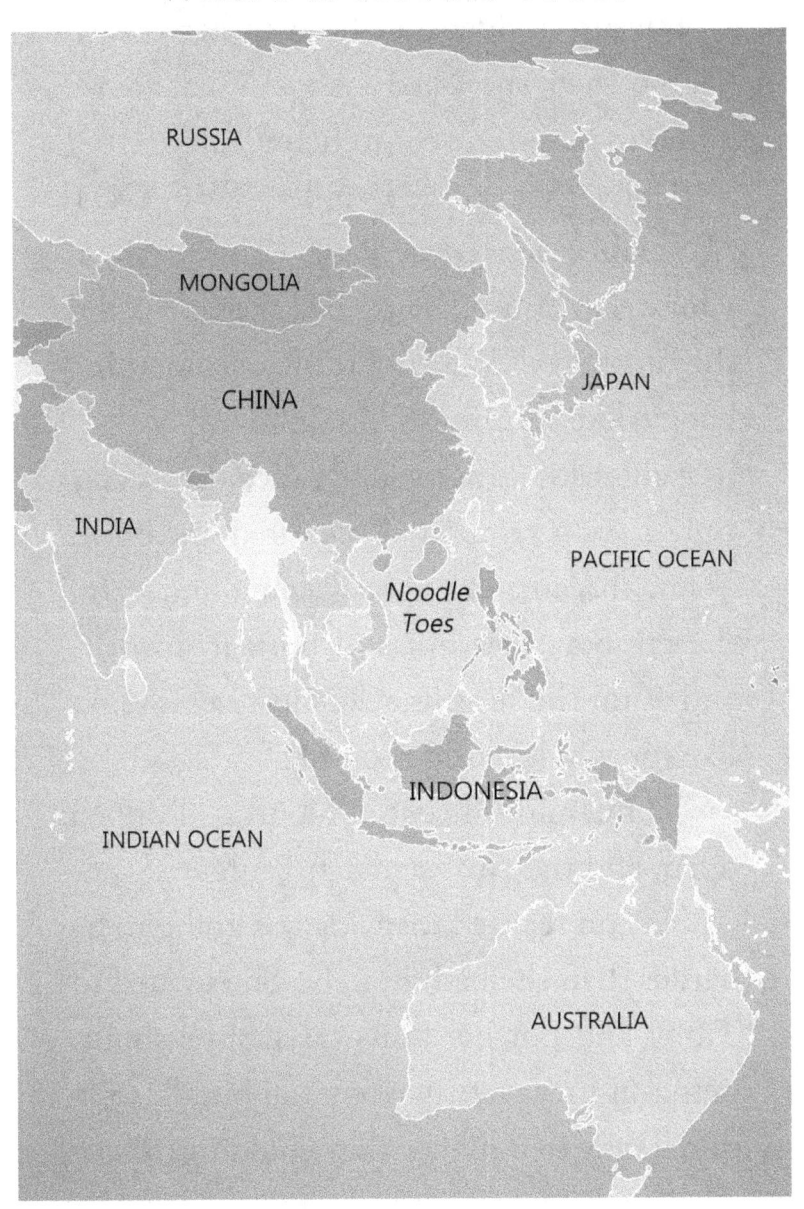

Hiccup nodded her head to agree with Tibby. Then, she asked Tibby, "What are we going to do—*hiccup*—to help Paul?"

Tibby gave a wide smile. "I'VE GOT IT!" Tibby looked at Paul. "This is all in your head. You're having bad thoughts, and they aren't real. Why not think of something happy, like sunshine and rainbows?"

Paul said, "That sounds nice, but every time I see a rainbow, I see a red ant on it. Then, the ant's friends all come and carry the rainbow to a hut and burn it down… and as for the sunshine, let's just say it looks like the whole world is on fire."

Tibby and Hiccup's mouths dropped open, and they just stared at Paul.

Hiccup realized that this was going to be harder than she had thought. She turned to Tibby and put her arms on Tibby's shoulders as if they were in a football huddle. She told Tibby that maybe they could introduce

46

a small animal to Paul first. Once he was comfortable with the small animal, they could bring an animal that was a little larger until they built up to an even larger animal. Hiccup told Tibby they needed to first look for something small and cute… like a little mouse.

"Paul, Tibby is going to bring a tiny, cute mouse. A very, very nice mouse," said Hiccup calmly.

Paul's eyes grew big, and he wanted to slither off, but Hiccup talked him into staying. As Paul sat there waiting, Tibby slowly walked over with the cutest little white mouse. Tibby was holding it by its tail and dangling it. The mouse squirmed and said to Tibby, "Please don't let him eat me. I'm too young to die."

Hiccup said, "See Paul, this cute little mouse—*hiccup*—is scared of you."

Paul looked at the mouse's eyes. "Hiccup,

they are evil, *red eyes*, with fire burning in them." Paul thought the mouse had the power to emit fire laser beams from his eyes, and of course, Paul thought those eyes could burn down a hut with him inside it.

Hiccup explained that they were just red and that was all. They were not evil, and there was no fire burning.

At this point, the mouse passed out.

A surprised Paul looked right at Hiccup and said, "Did I do that?"

"Yes, you did," responded Hiccup.

Hiccup was relieved that Paul did not run away after seeing the mouse. She told Tibby to go find Paul a bird and to make sure it was colorful and beautiful. That way, the bird would not seem so scary to Paul.

While Tibby was looking for a bird, Paul was afraid because they made loud, chirping sounds. He slithered slowly through the leaves and then blended in with the ground and disappeared. He was watching from afar.

Tibby came back, but not with a bird. He had a jaguar with him.

"What happened with making sure—*hiccup*—you bring a colorful and beautiful bird?" asked a frustrated Hiccup.

Tibby said, "I couldn't get one. Every bird I went up to flew away. And then. I ran into this nice jaguar and asked if she would come over."

"Miss Jaguar," Tibby asked in front of Hiccup, "Are you afraid of Paul the King Cobra?"

"NO!" said the jaguar. Then, one second later, her voice cracked and she said, "Is he… is he… is he here?" looking around for Paul.

Paul came out of his hiding place, and the jaguar did not move. She looked at him and froze like a statue. Tibby tapped her on

the shoulder, as if he was snapping her out of a spell. She let out a shrieking meow.

Tibby said with disbelief, "I thought I was the only one who meowed."

The jaguar screamed, "IT'S PAUL THE KING COBRA! I'M OUT OF HERE!"

"Did I do that?" asked Paul with surprise.

"Yes, you did," responded Hiccup.

Tibby went back and finally found a bird, and the bird was afraid of Paul. Hiccup told Tibby to go find something bigger. Tibby found a monkey, and the monkey was afraid of Paul too. Then, Hiccup told Tibby, "Go find something even bigger." Tibby found a crocodile, who wanted to appear like a tough guy. But when he saw Paul, he wanted nothing to do with him. He quickly crawled away.

"See, Paul, I don't think you're seeing what we're all seeing," said Hiccup. And in a strong voice, she said, "You're not Paul the

Paranoid Snake. YOU ARE PAUL THE KING COBRA OF THE JUNGLE!"

Tibby had a confused look and said, "Hiccup, I thought I was the king of the jungle."

Hiccup gave Tibby a look—a look that said, "*Be quiet, Tibby. You're not helping.*"

Paul's eyes lit up. His fears were going away. He did not feel so afraid anymore after seeing how scared the animals were of him. He was so grateful to have met Tibby and Hiccup and thanked them for giving him his new title: Paul the King Cobra of the Jungle.

With kind eyes, Hiccup looked at Tibby. She wanted to give him a new title too. "Why don't we just call you Tibby the Tiger instead of Tibby the *Chubby* Tiger?"

Tibby smiled. "I like the sound of that."

It was now time for Hiccup and Tibby to get back home to Coconut Desert Island.

Before saying goodbye to Paul, Hiccup asked him where they might find a river. Paul pointed to the north. He told them they could not miss it because the large river ran right through Noodle Toes.

As Tibby and Hiccup walked to the river, it started to rain. Looking up, Tibby said, "Hmm, the raindrops do look like giant big toes."

They found the river, and Hiccup got into the cool water. She dunked underwater and popped her eyes out. She started to think of home and let out a hiccup, and a bubble started to glow. It was bright orange and started to get bigger and bigger and bigger. It was now time to go back to Coconut Desert Island.

CHAPTER 7
Hiccupping Portals

Tibby and Hiccup were glad to be home, but they still did not know where Benny was. Moreover, they could not find Charlize anywhere on Coconut Desert Island either, which was very strange. The same giant green beetle that Charlize was afraid of overheard Tibby and Hiccup. He told them that Charlize went through a glowing, purple light tunnel. At that moment, Tibby and Hiccup realized that Charlize had entered the left portal and guessed that Benny must be there too. They needed to somehow find them.

Tibby asked Hiccup, "Do you have any ideas?"

"Yes, but I don't know—*hiccup*—if it will work," responded a worried Hiccup.

Hiccup explained that she could open portals and see if Charlize and Benny were there. It could take days or weeks, and they might not find them. Tibby said that it was worth a try.

Each time Hiccup opened a portal, she and Tibby would go inside. They would look around, and they would spend a day asking the locals if they had seen Charlize and Benny. But no one had seen them.

Hiccup kept trying. They entered more portals. In one portal, they saw the Tooth Fairy counting teeth. In another portal, they walked upon Santa Claus sneaking behind a Christmas tree to eat cookies. In another portal, they saw the Easter Bunny secretly dipping his carrots into chocolate.

But at the close of every visit, they returned to Coconut Desert Island without Charlize and Benny.

Tibby was beginning to feel very sad, and he realized how much he missed both of them, especially Benny.

Hiccup still kept trying. In another portal, they slid down a rainbow into a pot of gold. Standing there was a little bearded man. He was wearing a green coat and a hat that had a belt buckle on it—a leprechaun, he called himself.

Hiccup and Tibby told him they were trying to find their friends. The leprechaun said he was able to see the future and that an animal who looked just like Tibby was going to be of help. Tibby and Hiccup thought the bearded man was a little crazy and ignored him, so they headed back to Coconut Desert Island.

Hiccup said sadly, "Let's try one more

portal tomorrow morning."

Tibby and Hiccup entered the last portal. When they entered, they saw rolling green hills covered with tall, thick grass. A stream with trees and bushes along the sides was running through the land. Tibby and Hiccup were looking at the beautiful scene, but then, they were startled when they heard a *hiss*.

"Not again," said Tibby.

With four hiccups, Hiccup said, "Let's hope it's not another king cobra because I'm pretty sure this one will not be afraid of us."

They saw an orange-yellow snake with brown stripes on him. The snake looked at Tibby and Hiccup. He smiled and said, "G'day, mate. I'm Ty the Tiger Snake."

Tibby said, "A tiger. You look just like me, except you are way thinner and not as hairy."

With a hiss, Ty the Tiger Snake said,

"You're right. We look alike."

Hiccup's eyes grew big. "Tibby, the leprechaun said there would be an animal that looks just like you who would help us."

"You're right, Hiccup!" said a very happy Tibby.

Tibby asked Ty if he had seen Benny and Charlize. Tibby began to describe them to Ty.

Ty said, "I saw a girl cat who was superfast—faster than any other kangaroo I've ever seen. She had a bumblebee with her. I got to say, what an odd pair they are."

With excitement, Tibby said, "HICCUP, CHARLIZE AND BENNY ARE HERE!"

"Now, we have to find them," said Hiccup to Tibby. Then, she whispered, "Let's get out of here quickly. Ty reminds me of Paul, except I'm certain this guy is looking at me like I'm a big piece of steak that he wants to eat."

"THANK YOU, TY!" yelled Hiccup, as they quickly walked away.

"Hiccup, which way do we go?" asked Tibby.

Hiccup noticed that on the ground there was an arrow made of branches and rocks. She was not sure what it meant but thought they should follow it. "Come on, Tibby, let's—*hiccup*—go this way."

Then, they saw another arrow and then another arrow. They kept following the arrows until they ended up on the coast of the island.

"Now what, Hiccup? There aren't any more arrows," said Tibby.

Hiccup said, "We wait."

And so, they waited and waited. Then, they waited some more. And then… Tibby from a distance saw a familiar dark shape over the horizon that looked just like Charlize… and it was Charlize with Benny on her head!

"CHARLIZE, WE ARE HERE!" hollered Tibby. "RIGHT HERE! OVER HERE!"

Before Tibby could say another word, Hiccup

began to run to them. Tibby had no idea Hiccup could run that fast. Tibby ran after her. Charlize ran toward them as Benny yelled, "WE'RE COMING!" They gave each other one big bear hug. At last, they were all together.

"I missed you, Tibby," said Benny with a tear.

Tibby put Benny on his shoulder and then thanked Charlize for taking care of his best friend. Then, he said, "We've been looking for you guys for weeks. We thought we would never find you."

Charlize smiled. "But you did, and that's all that matters."

And with a hiccup, Hiccup said, "Let's get out of here, shall we?"